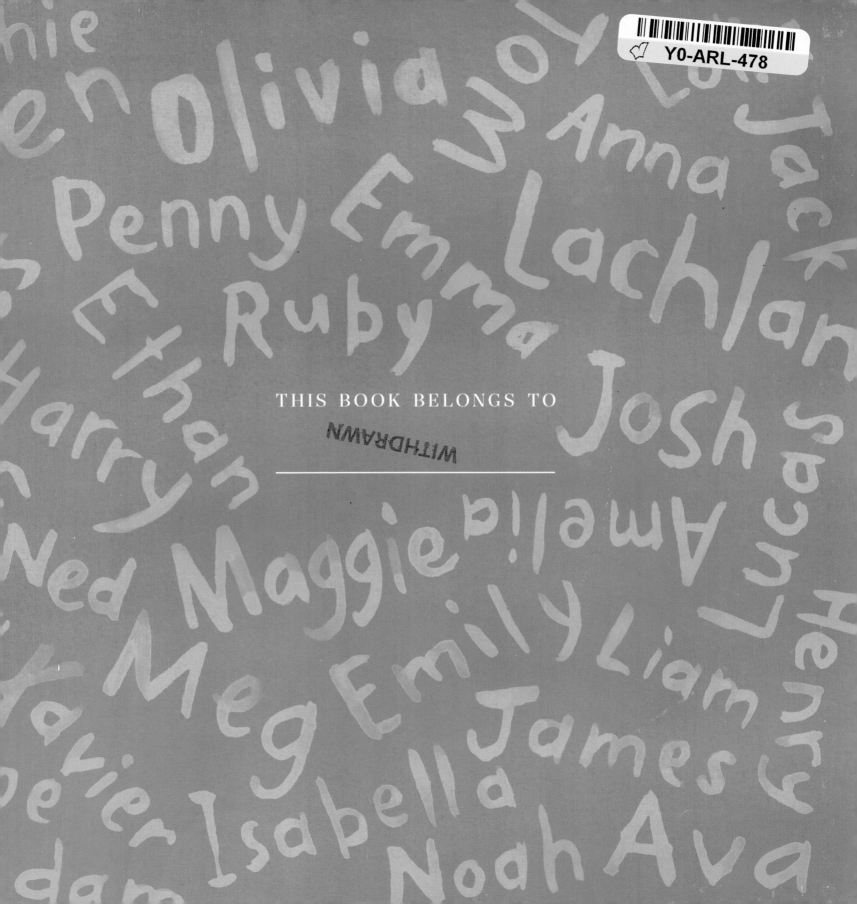

THIS BOOK BELONGS TO

WITHDRAWN

WE WISH YOU A RIPPER CHRISTMAS

Colin & Greg would like to dedicate 'We Wish You A Ripper Christmas' to Aussies, young and old, far and wide, who continue to sing along with Bucko & Champs every Christmas.

To Will and Ollie—Roland Harvey

Scholastic Australia
345 Pacific Highway Lindfield NSW 2070
An imprint of Scholastic Australia Pty Limited
PO Box 579 Gosford NSW 2250
ABN 11 000 614 577
www.scholastic.com.au

Part of the Scholastic Group
Sydney • Auckland • New York • Toronto • London • Mexico City
• New Delhi • Hong Kong • Buenos Aires • Puerto Rico

Published by Scholastic Australia in 2013.
All words by Colin Buchanan and Greg Champion © 2013 Universal Music Publishing Australia P/L.
Illustrations copyright © Roland Harvey, 2013.

National Library of Australia Cataloguing-in-Publication entry
Author: Buchanan, Colin, 1964- author.
Title: We wish you a ripper christmas / written by Colin Buchanan & Greg Champion; illustrated by Roland Harvey.
ISBN: 978 1 74283 723 9 (hardback)
Target Audience: For pre-school age.
Subjects: Animals—Australia—Juvenile fiction.
Lost and found possessions—Juvenile fiction.
Christmas stories, Australian.
Other Authors/Contributors: Champion, Greg, author.
Harvey, Roland, 1945- illustrator.
Dewey Number: A823.4

Typeset in Narziss Drops, featuring Mailart Rubberstamp.

Printed in China by RR Donnelley.
Scholastic Australia's policy, in association with RR Donnelley, is to use papers that are renewable and made efficiently from wood grown in sustainable forests, so as to minimise its environmental footprint.

10 9 8 7 6 5 4 3 2 1   13 14 15 16 17 / 1

WE WISH YOU A RIPPER CHRISTMAS

Written by Colin Buchanan & Greg Champion

Illustrated by Roland Harvey

A SCHOLASTIC AUSTRALIA BOOK

We wish you a **RIPPER CHRISTMAS**,

A full-bore ripper Christmas,

A deadset ripper Christmas,

And a **SNAPPY** New Year!

Now who can you see,

Up there in his sleigh?

I think **SANTA WOMBAT**

Is heading our way.

The good girls and boys

Know they won't be missed,

If old **SANTA WOMBAT**

Hangs onto his list.

But out near the windmill,

Up over the trees,

OH NO! Santa's list

Flutters off on the breeze.

'HELP!' Santa cries out,

All red-faced and puffed.

'If I don't find that list, well,

No stockings get stuffed!'

We wish you a **RIPPER CHRISTMAS**,

A full-bore ripper Christmas,

A deadset ripper Christmas,

And a **SNAPPY** New Year!

He **SCOURED** under sheds,

While the gangly emus

Played Christmas Eve **CRICKET**

With the red kangaroos.

He **SEARCHED** for his list
On that hot summer night,
While koalas hung tinsel
And **CHRISTMAS TREE LIGHTS**.

The dingos were wrapping up

BRIGHT coloured thongs,

As Santa looked all round

The **BIG** billabong.

'CRIKEY!' cried Santa,

As rock star galahs

Played 'FAH LAH LAH RUM PUM'

On electric guitars.

The possums were JINGLING

Their tails in a twist.

'I'M DONE FOR!' cried Santa,

'If I don't find my list!'

We wish you a **RIPPER CHRISTMAS**,

A full-bore ripper Christmas,

A deadset ripper Christmas,

And a **SNAPPY** New Year!

Then **MR GOANNA**,

With music in hand,

Stood, ready to strike up

The carols-night band.

'**STOP!**' Santa Wombat

cried out, fingers crossed,

'Mixed up in your music's

The **LIST** that I lost!'

'The children are in for

A **BEAUT** Christmas Day!

Bonza,' laughed Santa,

'Now, **UP AND AWAY!**'

The animals cheered

And the **CHRISTMAS BELLS RANG,**

As Aussies right over

AUSTRALIA all sang . . .

We wish you a **RIPPER CHRISTMAS**,

A full-bore ripper Christmas,

A deadset ripper Christmas,

And a **SNAPPY** New Year!

Claire Todd Lucy Wil S
Charlie Tim Lucy Matt
Charlotte Motilda
Lily Ella Bel Sam Max
Pip Harriet Jon Hetty
Mike Holly Syd Dolly Co
Cecil Rip Lily
Cooper Sus
Lolly Ollie Lena Mia
Paul Betsy Eva Polly